Is it too small?

An Ivy and Mack story

T0313546

Written by Juliet Clare Bell

Illustrated by Gustavo Mazali

with Szépvölgyi Eszter

Collins

What's in this story?

Listen and say

autumn

conker

leaves

Download the audio at www.collins.co.uk/839654

hedgehog

🎧 It was a nice afternoon in autumn. Ivy and Mack looked at the beautiful leaves with Mum and Dad.

"I *like* green leaves," said Mack, "but red and orange leaves are my favourites!"

Ivy looked at Mack's conkers.

"Why do you need all *those*?" asked Ivy.

"Conkers are my *favourite*!" said Mack.

Ivy saw a mountain of dry leaves. "Let's jump, Mack!" she said.

"Jumping in leaves is my *favourite*!" said Mack.

Mack saw some more leaves. "Look, Ivy! This mountain of leaves is *BIGGER*!"

"The leaves are moving! Mack, STOP!" Ivy called.

"Wow!" said Ivy. There was a very small hedgehog under the leaves.

The hedgehog was a baby. "Where's its mummy?" asked Mack.

They looked in the leaves. "Where can she be?" asked Ivy.

"Look! Helen's Hedgehog Hospital," said Mum.

"Can we call them?" asked Ivy.

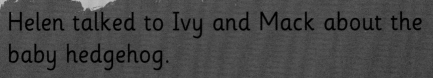

Helen talked to Ivy and Mack about the baby hedgehog.

"What can we do?" asked Ivy.

"Put it in a box, so it isn't cold. And bring it to the hedgehog hospital," said Helen.

"We need the car," said Dad.

"And a box," said Mum.

The hedgehog made a '*peep*' noise.

"*Peep* is a good name for it," said Mack.

"My conkers," said Mack.
Ivy helped Mack find all his conkers.

They turned round. Peep was gone!

"Where are you, Peep?" called Mack.

Ivy looked up. "Hedgehogs can't climb trees!"

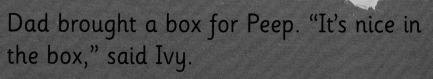

Dad brought a box for Peep. "It's nice in the box," said Ivy.

"There's Peep!" said Mack. "Quick, Mum!"

Mum put on some gloves, picked up the hedgehog, and put it in the box. Then they gave Peep some water.

Helen's Hedgehog Hospital was in a big house. Helen put Peep's box on a long table.

"This is Peep," said Ivy.

"Hello, Peep! Are you hungry?" said Helen. "Would you like to feed it?"

Mack looked in the bowls. "Can Peep eat these?" asked Mack.

"No, Mack," said Helen.

"Why not? Is it too small?" said Mack.

"Yes," said Helen. "Bigger hedgehogs can eat them. Babies need milk."

Mack fed Peep some goat's milk.

"Hedgehogs can't drink cow's milk,"
Helen told Mack and Ivy. "But they like
goat's milk."

"Mum and Dad! Come and see!" said Ivy.

Helen took Peep into the garden.

"Peep can play here," she said.

"You've got *lots* of hedgehogs," Ivy said.

"Why can't we have Peep?" said Mack. "Peep's my *favourite*."

"I'm sorry, Mack," said Helen. "Hedgehogs aren't pets."

At home, Ivy and Mack were sad.

"Do you want to play with these?" said Ivy. "They are your favourite."

"*Peep* is my favourite," said Mack.

Then Ivy had an idea ...

... to make a family of conker hedgehogs.

Ivy laughed. "It's a family of Peeps!"

"You're my *favourite*," said Mack.

Ivy looked at Mack. "Which hedgehog do you mean?"

"*I mean you, Ivy!*"

Picture dictionary

Listen and repeat

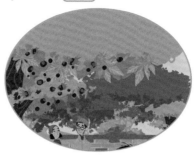

autumn

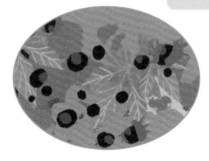

conker

hedgehog

leaf

leaves

1 Look and order the story

2 Listen and say

Collins

Published by Collins
An imprint of HarperCollins*Publishers*
Westerhill Road
Bishopbriggs
Glasgow
G64 2QT

HarperCollins*Publishers*
1st Floor, Watermarque Building
Ringsend Road
Dublin 4
Ireland

William Collins' dream of knowledge for all began with the publication of his first book in 1819.

A self-educated mill worker, he not only enriched millions of lives, but also founded a flourishing publishing house. Today, staying true to this spirit, Collins books are packed with inspiration, innovation and practical expertise. They place you at the centre of a world of possibility and give you exactly what you need to explore it.

10 9 8 7 6 5 4 3

ISBN 978-0-00-839654-1

Collins® and COBUILD® are registered trademarks of HarperCollins*Publishers* Limited

www.collins.co.uk/elt

Author: Juliet Clare Bell
Lead illustrator: Gustavo Mazali (Beehive)
Copy illustrator: Szépvölgyi Eszter (Beehive)
Series editor: Rebecca Adlard
Commissioning editor: Zoë Clarke
Publishing manager: Lisa Todd
Product managers: Jennifer Hall and Caroline Green
In-house editor: Alma Puts Keren
Project manager: Emily Hooton
Editor: Deborah Friedland
Proofreaders: Natalie Murray and Michael Lamb
Cover designer: Kevin Robbins
Typesetter: 2Hoots Publishing Services Ltd
Audio produced by id audio, London
Reading guide author: Julie Penn
Production controller: Rachel Weaver
Printed and bound in UK by Pureprint

MIX
Paper from
responsible sources
FSC www.fsc.org   **FSC™ C007454**

This book is produced from independently certified FSC™ paper to ensure responsible forest management.

For more information visit: **www.harpercollins.co.uk/green**

Download the audio for this book and a reading guide for parents and teachers at www.collins.co.uk/839654